ALBERT HELPS OUT

by **Eleanor May** • Illustrated by **Deborah Melmon**

THE KANE PRESS / NEW YORK

To Nadia, for all your helping out over the years!—E.M.

Acknowledgments: We wish to thank the following people for their helpful advice and review of the material contained in this book: Susan Longo, Former Early Childhood and Elementary School Teacher, Mamaroneck, NY; and Rebeka Eston Salemi, Kindergarten Teacher, Lincoln School, Lincoln, MA.

Special thanks to Susan Longo for providing the Fun Activities in the back of this book.

Library of Congress Cataloging-in-Publication Data

Names: May, Eleanor, author. | Melmon, Deborah, illustrator.
Title: Albert helps out / by Eleanor May ; illustrated by Deborah Melmon.
Description: New York : Kane Press, 2017. | Series: Mouse math | Summary: "In this story about counting money, Albert the mouse needs two quarters to use the library's new penny-smashing machine. Luckily, Wanda has a great idea for how Albert can earn the money"— Provided by publisher.
Identifiers: LCCN 2016024832 (print) | LCCN 2016047814 (ebook) | ISBN 9781575658575 (reinforced library binding : alk. paper) | ISBN 9781575658605 (paperback : alk. paper) | ISBN 9781575658636 (ebook)
Subjects: | CYAC: Money—Fiction. | Coins—Fiction. | Counting—Fiction. | Moneymaking projects—Fiction. | Mice—Fiction.
Classification: LCC PZ7.M4513 Ajh 2017 (print) | LCC PZ7.M4513 (ebook) | DDC [E]—dc23
LC record available at https://lccn.loc.gov/2016024832

1 3 5 7 9 10 8 6 4 2

First published in the United States of America in 2017 by Kane Press, Inc.
Printed in China

Book Design: Edward Miller

Mouse Math is a registered trademark of Kane Press, Inc.

Visit us online at **www.kanepress.com**

 Like us on Facebook
facebook.com/kanepress

Follow us on Twitter
@KanePress

Dear Parent/Educator,

"I can't do math." Every child (or grownup!) who says these words has at some point along the way felt intimidated by math. For young children who are just being introduced to the subject, we wanted to create a world in which math was not simply numbers on a page, but a part of life—an adventure!

Enter Albert and Wanda, two little mice who live in the walls of a People House. Children will be swept along with this irrepressible duo and their merry band of friends as they tackle mouse-sized problems and dilemmas (and sometimes *cat-sized* problems and dilemmas!).

Each book in the **MOUSE MATH**® series provides a fresh take on a basic math concept. The mice discover solutions as they, for instance, use position words while teaching a pet snail to do tricks or count the alarmingly large number of friends they've invited over on a rainy day—and, lo and behold, they are doing math!

Math educators who specialize in early childhood learning have applied their expertise to make sure each title is as helpful as possible to young children—and to their parents and teachers. Fun activities at the ends of the books and on our website encourage kids to think and talk about math in ways that will make each concept clear and memorable.

As with our award-winning Math Matters® series, our aim is to captivate children's imaginations by drawing them into the story, and so into the math at the heart of each adventure. It is our hope that kids will want to hear and read the **MOUSE MATH** stories again and again and that, as they grow up, they will approach math with enthusiasm and see it as an invaluable tool for navigating the world they live in.

Sincerely,

Joanne Kane

Joanne E. Kane
Publisher

The library had a brand-new machine.
"What is it?" Albert asked.

"It's a penny smasher," his sister, Wanda, explained.
"You put a penny in and turn the crank. The penny
comes out flat, with a new picture on it."

"I have a penny!" Albert said. "Can I get a picture of Captain Slime?"

Wanda read the sign. "You need two quarters, too."

CRASH!

"Oh, dear," said Dr. Crumble, the librarian, looking at the books she'd dropped.

Albert helped her pick them up.

"What a good helper you are, Albert!" Dr. Crumble said.

"I like to help," Albert said.

Captain Slime

New

Captain Slime
Snail Sets Sail

Book 2

On the way out, Albert asked, "Where can I get two quarters?"

"Dr. Crumble said you're a good helper," Wanda said.
"You could earn money by helping someone out." She stopped.
"Would you open the door? My arms are full of books."

"How much will you pay me?" Albert asked.

"Albert!" Wanda said. "That's NOT the kind of help I meant!"

A **penny** = 1 cent.

A **nickel** = 5 cents.

A **dime** = 10 cents.

A **quarter** = 25 cents.

9

At home, Wanda sat down to read.

"Would you pay me to do your homework?" Albert asked.

"Or I could make you a super-duper special snack."

"No, thanks," Wanda said.

"I know!" Albert offered. "I can sing your favorite song!"

"How about just sitting quietly?" Wanda asked.
"I'll give you one cent for every minute that you
let me read in peace."

Albert sat down. He waited . . .

And waited . . .

And waited.

Finally, Wanda shut her book.
Albert jumped up. "How many minutes was I quiet?
A hundred? A thousand?"

Wanda looked at her watch. "Four."

Wanda got her piggy bank and counted out the pennies. "One, two, three, four."

"Now I have five pennies," Albert said. "Does that equal two quarters?"

"No, but you can trade five pennies for a nickel," Wanda said.

1¢ + 1¢ + 1¢ + 1¢ + 1¢ = 5¢

Albert took the nickel. "Want me to be quiet while you read another book?"

"I can't afford it," Wanda said. "Why don't you go ask if the neighbors need any help?"

Albert knocked on Mrs. Nibble's door.

"Hello, Albert!" Mrs. Nibble said. "My cheese biscuits just came out of the oven. Would you like to help me eat them?"

"Is that the kind of help you pay for?" Albert asked.
Mrs. Nibble looked confused.

"I'm trying to earn money," Albert explained. "Wanda said to ask if you need any help."

Mrs. Nibble smiled. "I'll pay you a nickel to take Ringo for a walk."

RINGO

On the way out, Albert ran into their neighbor Mr. Squeak.
"I'm walking Ringo for Mrs. Nibble," Albert said.
"She's going to pay me a nickel."

Mr. Squeak asked, "Could you walk Lady, too?
I'll even pay you in advance!"

"Now I have two nickels!" Albert said. "Does that equal a quarter?"

Mr. Squeak shook his head. "Sorry. But you can trade two nickels for a dime."

5¢   +   5¢   =   10¢

Outside, Albert heard howls. Then he saw his cousin Pete. "Babysitting the Mousely triplets?" Albert asked.

Pete nodded. "They wouldn't take turns on the slide."

"LADY! RINGO!" the triplets yelled.

"You can hold their leashes," Albert said. "IF you take turns."

"You saved the day!" said Cousin Pete. "I'm getting paid to babysit, so you should too." He gave Albert a dime.

"Now I have two dimes!" Albert said. "Does that equal a quarter?"

"Almost," said Cousin Pete.

10¢ + 10¢ = 20¢

Albert dropped off Lady and Ringo.

Mrs. Nibble gave Albert a nickel.

"Now I have two dimes and a nickel," he said.

"You can trade that for a quarter," Mrs. Nibble said.

"I CAN?" Albert exclaimed.

20¢   +   5¢   =   25¢

"What are you going to spend it on?" asked Mrs. Nibble.

"I'm saving up to try the penny smasher at the library," Albert said. "I need two quarters, so I'm halfway there."

Mrs. Nibble smiled. "In that case, here's another quarter. That money helps the library buy books. It's a good cause."

"Wow, thanks!" Albert said.

24

"Look, Wanda!" Albert said, dashing inside.
"I have two quarters! Can we go back to the library?"

"Sure!" Wanda said. "While you were gone, I finished all my books."

25¢ + 25¢ = 50¢

At the library, Albert made a beeline for the penny smasher. He put his two quarters in the slots and—

"Oh, NO!" Albert said. "I have two quarters. But I don't have a penny anymore!"

"A penny for my helper Albert?" Dr. Crumble said.
"I think I can help with—"

CRASH!

Albert helped Dr. Crumble pick up the books.
Then he took the penny.

"I guess I owe you another penny now," joked Dr. Crumble.

Albert smiled. "I don't need another penny. . . ."

"I like to help!"

▲ 2 FUN ACTIVITIES ❸ 4

Albert Helps Out supports children's understanding of **identifying and counting money**, important concepts in early math learning. Use the activities below to extend the math topic and to support children's early reading skills.

🐭 ENGAGE

▸ Begin by displaying the cover of the book and asking the children what they think this story may be about. As the children share their ideas, be sure to repeat or paraphrase them as you record them on a board or on easel paper. Refer back to their ideas at the end of the story.

▸ Ask the children to raise their hands if they have ever had to save their money to buy something they really wanted. Have them share what it was and what they did to save up for it.

▸ Now it's time to read the story and find out how Albert discovers ways to earn money to buy something special!

🐭 LOOK BACK

▸ After reading the story, ask the children if they can recap the story in their own words. What happens in the beginning of the story, in the middle, and at the end?

▸ Now ask the children: *How much money did Albert need for the penny smasher? Who can remember the names of all the different coins Albert earned in this story? How much was each coin worth?* (Write the name of each coin along with its value on a board or on easel paper for reference.)

▸ Have each child turn to a partner and discuss what lessons Albert learned in this story. Ask the children to share their thoughts with the whole group. Now ask: *In what ways can you be helpful to other people?* Have the children turn to their partners again to think of several ways. Then have them share their thoughts with the group.

🐭 TRY THIS!

Bankers at Work

▶ Group the children in pairs and hand out bags of coins that include pennies, nickels, dimes, and quarters.

▶ Ask each group to come up with as many combinations as they can think of to make 25 cents.

▶ Ask the children to share their findings. Record all the different combinations on a board or on a large piece of paper.

▶ Repeat the same steps to make 50 cents.

Challenge: Ask the children to think up five combinations to make 100 cents, or $1.00. Record the different combinations.

🐭 THINK!

Let's play "TRADE-IN!"

▶ Before beginning this game, be sure to review with children the different combinations of coins that can add up to a value of 25 cents.

▶ Pair up the children and hand each pair a bag of coins that includes pennies, nickels, dimes, and quarters. Hand each group a die. Explain to them that they are to take turns rolling the die. Each time the die is rolled, the child may take that number of pennies from the bag. When they reach five pennies, they can trade them in for a nickel. When they reach two nickels, they can trade them in for a dime. When they reach two dimes and a nickel, they can trade them in for a quarter. The first child to trade in for a quarter is the winner!

▶ As the children become more familiar with trading in less valuable coins for more valuable coins, raise the winner's goal to 50 cents. Then to $1.00!

◆ **FOR MORE ACTIVITIES** ◆

visit www.kanepress.com/mouse-math-activities